## DATE DUE

|  |  |
|---|---|
|  |  |
|  |  |
|  |  |
|  |  |
|  |  |
|  |  |
|  |  |
|  |  |
|  |  |
|  |  |
|  |  |
|  |  |
|  |  |
|  |  |
|  |  |
|  |  |
| *CR* |  |
| GAYLORD | PRINTED IN U.S.A. |

# First Place Freddie

Peter Bently

Illustrated by Daniel Howarth

QEB Publishing

Freddie Flounder is going to the carnival.

His friend Sprat *whizzes* past.
"See you at the carnival, slowpoke!" calls Sprat.

"I wish I was as zippy as Sprat," thinks Freddie.

Angelfish nearly **bumps** into Freddie.

"Sorry, Freddie!" she says. "It's hard to see you in
all the mud and rocks and seaweed."

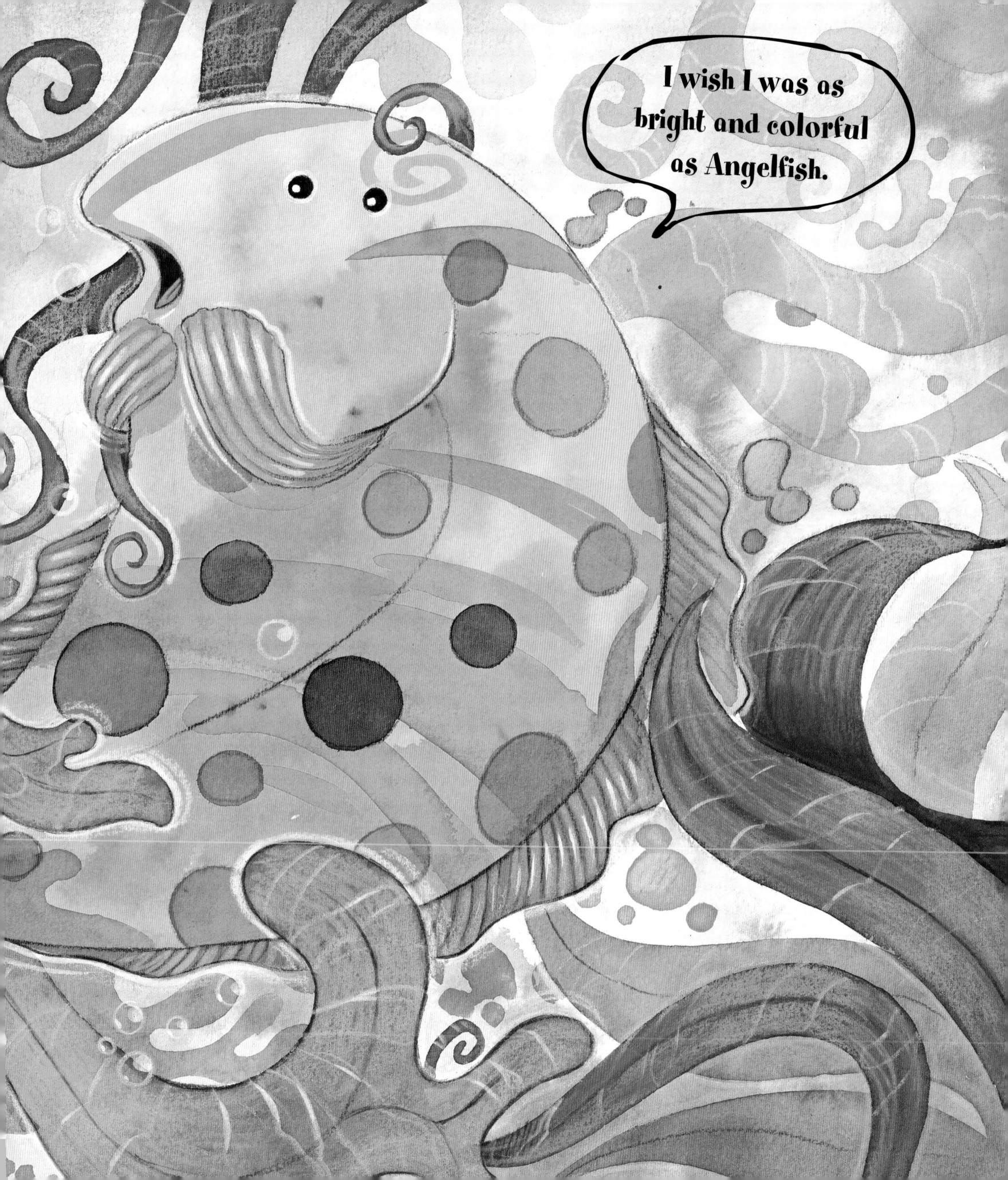

Pufferfish tumbles by and **puffs** himself up
like a big spiky balloon.
Everyone laughs.

"I wish I had a cool, fun shape
like Pufferfish," thinks Freddie.

Freddie and his friends have lots of fun at the carnival.

They ride on the Ferris wheel...

the merry-go-round...

the spiral slide...

and the bumper cars.

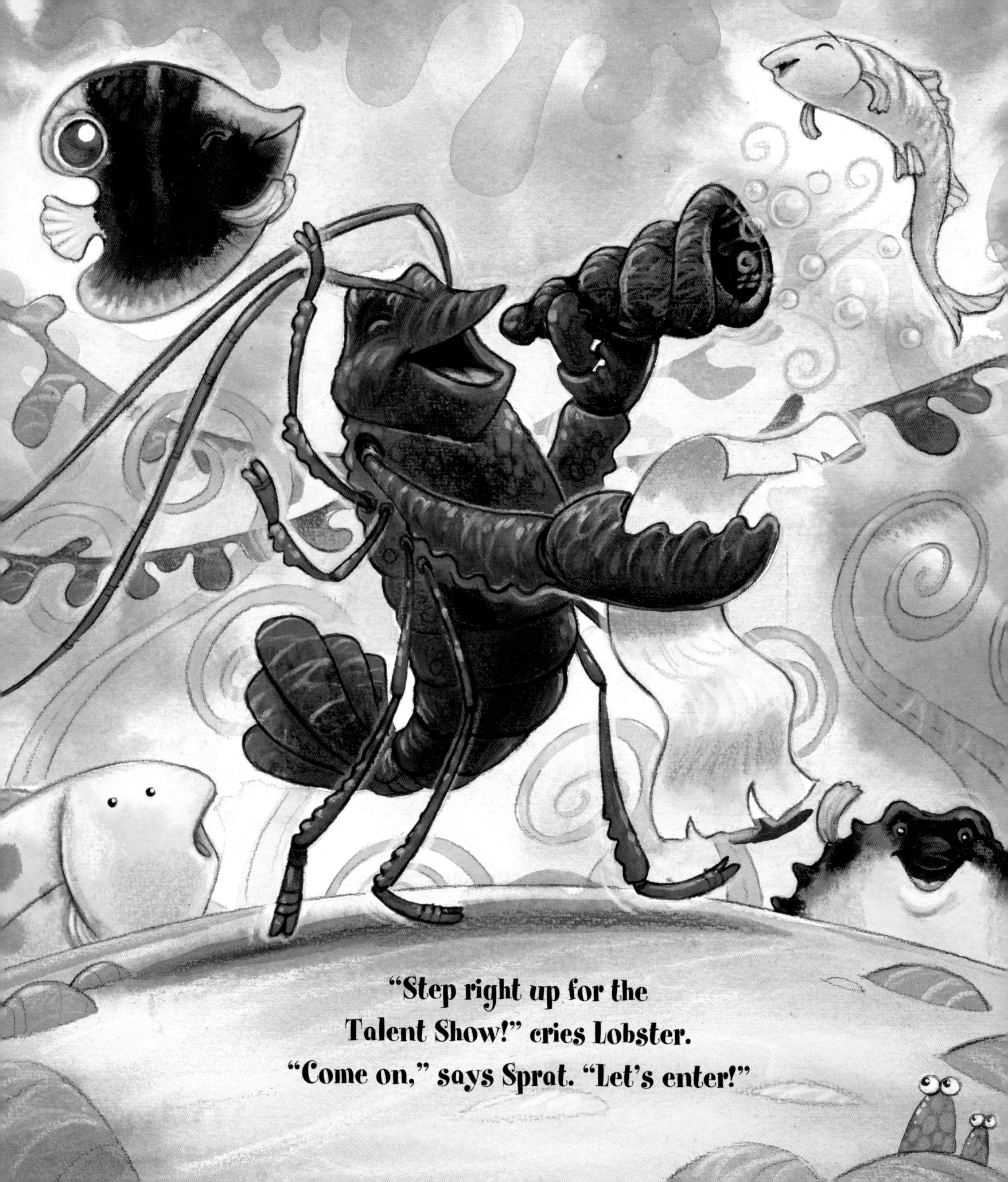

"Step right up for the
Talent Show!" cries Lobster.
"Come on," says Sprat. "Let's enter!"

Sprat enters
the competition
for the
FASTEST FISH,

Angelfish enters
the competition
for the MOST
COLORFUL FISH,

and Pufferfish enters the competition for the **FUNNiEST** FISH.

"Aren't you going to enter the Talent Show, Freddie?" asks Angelfish.

"There's no point," sighs Freddie, swimming sadly away. "I'm nobody special. Only a slow, dull, flat, boring fish."

Suddenly, Freddie's three friends *race* toward him.

"HELP!" cries Sprat. "Shark is coming!
I might be fast, but he's much faster than me!"

"If only I wasn't so colorful!" gasps Angelfish.
"**Shark** will spot me easily!"

"And me!" wails Pufferfish. "And I don't think he feels like laughing!"
"**Don't panic!**" says Freddie. "I've got an idea."

"Heh-heh!" cackles Shark. "I just saw some tasty-looking fish nipping behind that rock. It's time for my dinner!"

He swims closer,

and closer,

and **closer,**

and finds...

"Bah!" grumbles Shark. "Only mud and rocks and seaweed!"

And with a flick of his tail, he speeds off.

"**Phew!**" says Sprat.
"Thanks for hiding us, Freddie. That was close!"

Good job, Freddie!

"Let's get back to the carnival," says Sprat.
"Lobster is announcing the winners of the Talent Show!"

FASTEST FISH:
Sprat!
MOST COLORFUL FISH:
Angelfish!
FUNNIEST FISH:
Pufferfish!
1st
1st
1st

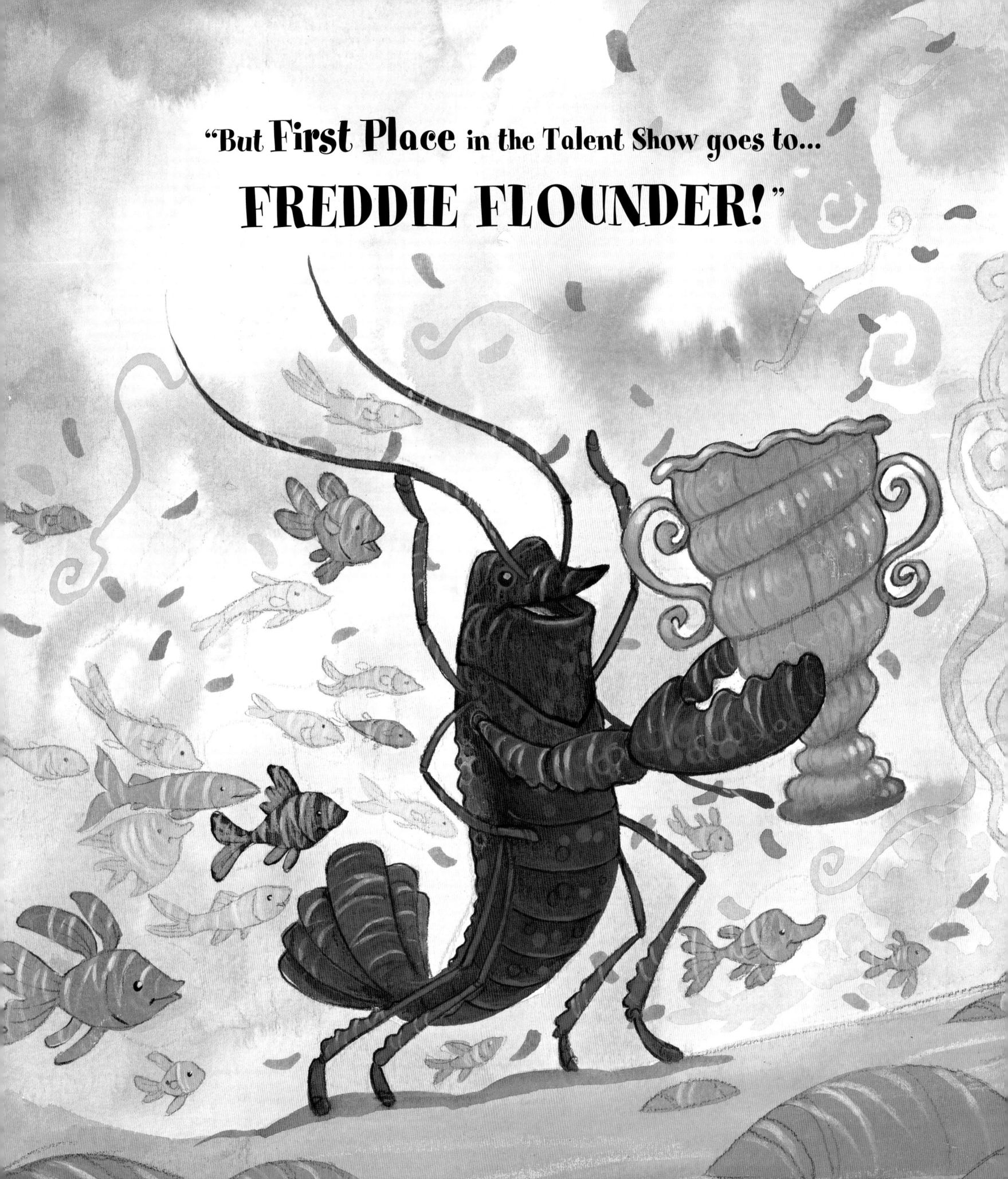

"For being the Best at Hiding
and the Best at Helping your Friends," says Lobster.

"Hooray for Freddie!" cheers Pufferfish.
"It's First Place for a Fantastic Flounder!"

# Notes for Parents and Teachers

- Look at the cover together before reading the book. Can the children guess what the story is about?

- Read the story, then ask the children to read it to you. Help them with any unfamiliar words and praise them for their efforts.

- Can the children remember all the different types of sea creatures in the story? Which ones are their favorites? Do they know where they live? Have they ever seen them in real life?

- Being different is an important topic in this story. Freddie thinks he is not special enough to win a prize. But in the end he saves his friends from the shark and wins the best prize of all. Ask the children what makes Freddie special (his camouflage, bravery, and quick thinking, or something else), and discuss how everyone is special in some way.

- Another key theme of the story is friendship. Discuss what the story tells children about being friends. What makes a good friend?

- Act out the story as a play. One child can be Freddie and four others can play his friends Pufferfish, Angelfish, and Sprat, and of course Shark. The other children can be all sorts of other fish and sea creatures. How do these fish and creatures move?

- Ask the children to draw and color in lots of different types of fish. They can draw real creatures or colorful fantasy fish. Cut the fish out and make a big collage.

Editor: Alexandra Koken
Designer: Chris Fraser

Copyright © QEB Publishing, Inc. 2011

Published in the United States by
QEB Publishing, Inc.
3 Wrigley, Suite A
Irvine, CA 92618

www.qed-publishing.co.uk

Library of Congress Cataloging-in-Publication Data

Bently, Peter.
First place Freddie / by Peter Bently ; illustrated by Daniel Howarth.
   p. cm. -- (Storytime)
 Summary: Freddie the flounder feels less talented than the other fish, but when a shark comes after his friends at the fair Freddie discovers his true worth.
 ISBN 978-1-60992-032-6 (library binding)
 [1. Self-perception--Fiction. 2. Ability--Fiction. 3. Fairs--Fiction. 4. Fishes--Fiction.] I. Howarth, Daniel, ill. II. Title.
 PZ7.B4475424To 2012
 [E]--dc22

                                    2011000340

ISBN 978 1 60992 032 6

Printed in China